A SERIOUS THOUGHT

Jonas Taul

GROUNDWOOD BOOKS
HOUSE OF ANANSI PRESS
TORONTO BERKELEY

THERE ONCE LIVED A LITTLE BOY.

One evening he was playing happily,
but then it was time for bed.

HE DRANK A GLASS OF MILK.

HE BRUSHED HIS TEETH.

HE CHANGED INTO HIS PAJAMAS AND CRAWLED INTO BED.

USUALLY HE FELL ASLEEP RIGHT AWAY, BUT NOT TONIGHT.
INSTEAD, HE STARTED TO THINK ALL KINDS OF THOUGHTS.

DANGEROUS THOUGHTS.

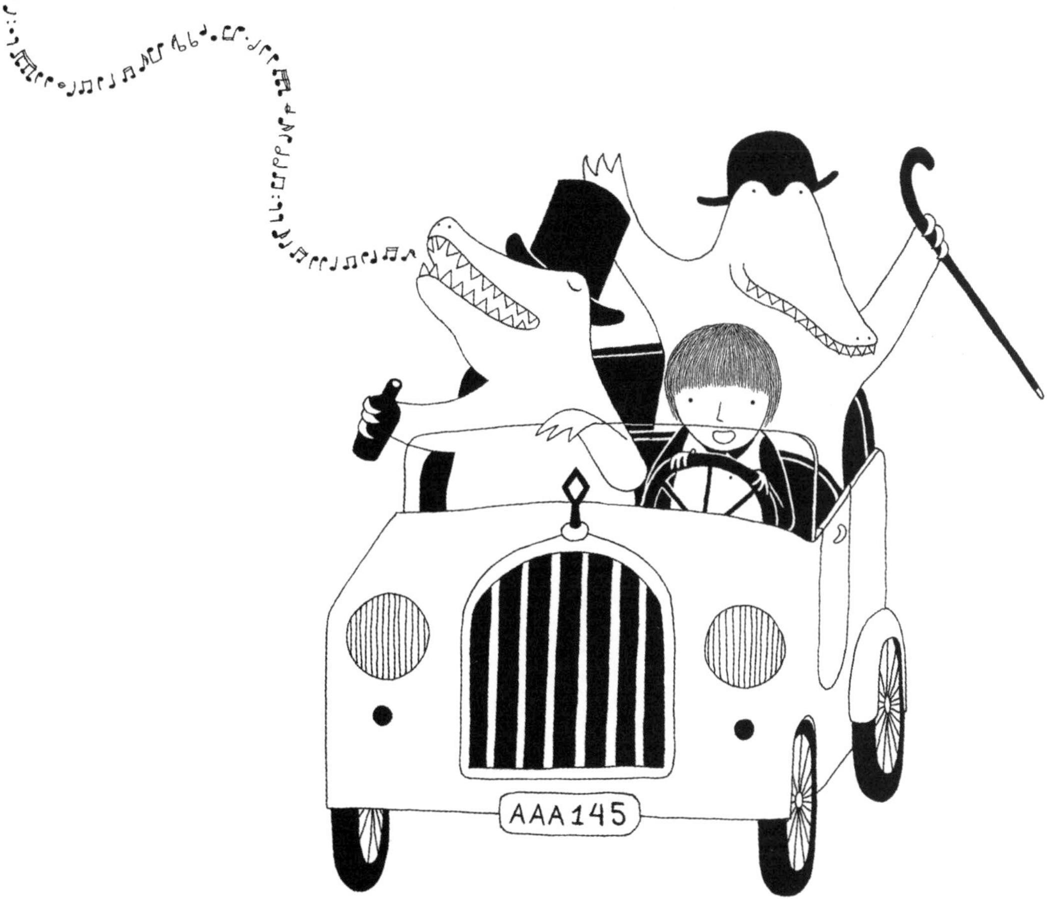
AAA145

ADMIRABLE THOUGHTS.

QUESTIONABLE THOUGHTS.

BEAUTIFUL THOUGHTS.

FRIGHTENING THOUGHTS.

THOUGHTS THAT REACHED FAR AND WIDE.

THEN A VERY SERIOUS THOUGHT CAME TO HIM. HE THOUGHT OF HOW OUR PLANET IS BUT A TINY MARBLE FLOATING IN ENDLESS EMPTY SPACE.

HE THOUGHT OF HOW HE WAS BUT ONE LITTLE BOY AMONG MANY OTHER CHILDREN, ALL LIVING SEPARATE LIVES UPON THIS LITTLE MARBLE.

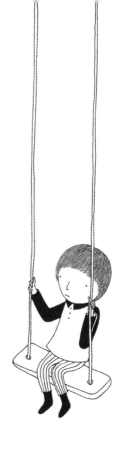

WHAT DID HE AND HIS DOINGS MATTER IN THE FACE OF SUCH INCREDIBLE GREATNESS?

ALL OF THIS MADE HIM VERY TIRED. HE CLOSED HIS EYES AND FELL ASLEEP, FEELING INCREDIBLY SMALL AND UNIMPORTANT.

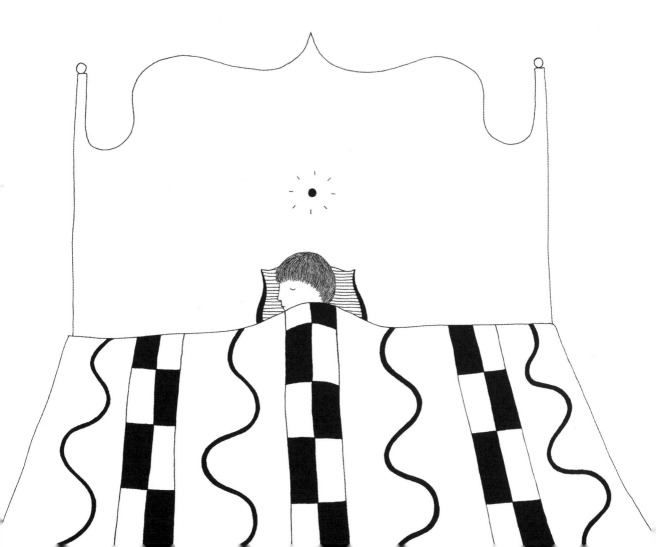

THE NIGHT WAS RESTLESS, FULL OF STRANGE AND PERPLEXING DREAMS.

IN THE MORNING, THE THOUGHTS WERE STILL ON HIS MIND.
THEY MADE HIM QUESTION THINGS.

PUZZLED, HE TURNED TO HIS FATHER FOR ADVICE, BUT HIS FATHER WAS TOO BUSY.

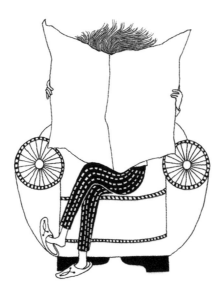

HE WENT OUTSIDE TO PLAY AND FORGET EVERYTHING,
YET NOTHING MADE HIM HAPPY.

HE DECIDED TO LEAVE THE GARDEN AND GO FOR A WALK.

HE WAS DEEP IN THOUGHT WHEN HE SUDDENLY REALIZED THAT HE WAS LOST AND ALONE IN THE MIDDLE OF A BIG FOREST.

A CAT APPEARED BEFORE HIM. IT WAS FRIENDLY AND SOFT.

HE FOLLOWED THE CAT, HOPING IT WOULD KNOW WHERE TO GO.

ON THE WAY, THEY NOTICED A LITTLE HEDGEHOG UNDERNEATH A FERN.
"THIS LITTLE FERN IS LIKE A BIG TREE NEXT TO THIS LITTLE HEDGEHOG,
AND NEXT TO ME, HE IS EVEN SMALLER. YET IT DOESN'T SEEM TO BOTHER HIM AT ALL."

THEY STOPPED BY A PUDDLE, AND A LITTLE FROG POPPED HIS HEAD OUT. SURPRISED, THE BOY THOUGHT TO HIMSELF, "MY, HOW SMALL THIS LITTLE FROG IS COMPARED TO ME AND MY GIANT REFLECTION, YET HE TRULY SEEMS HAPPY."

WANDERING ONWARD, THEY FOUND A NEST OF ANTS BY A BIG TREE.
THERE WERE SO MANY AND THEY WERE ALL BUSY BUILDING AND LIVING.
BEING INCREDIBLY TINY DIDN'T HINDER THEM AT ALL.

AT LAST THEY SAW A FAMILIAR HOUSE APPEAR IN THE DISTANCE.
WORRY HAD LEFT THE BOY'S HEART, AND HE NO LONGER FELT SMALL OR UNIMPORTANT.

ONCE AGAIN, IT WAS TIME FOR BED.